Strip Poker

Other playscripts by the same author in English

Comedy for 2

Running on empty

Comedies for 3

An Innocent Little Murder

Friday the 13th

Comedy for 4

Casket for two

Comedy for 5 or 6

Critical but stable

Comedy from 7 to 10

The Worst Village in England

Sketchs

Elle et Lui / Him and Her

JEAN-PIERRE MARTINEZ

Strip Poker

English translation by

Anne-Christine Gasc

La Comédi@thèque
comediatheque.com

Characters

Dave
Victoria
James
Pam

You must obtain the authorisations from the author prior to any public performance, whether by professional or amateur companies : comediatheque.com

ISBN 9781973346487

ACT ONE

Victoria, a blond, rather sexy, woman is in her living room. She is dressed up and is setting a fancy table for four. Her mobile rings. She takes the call.

Victoria (*pleasant*) – Hello…? (*Annoyed*) No, sorry, this isn't Dave, it's Victoria, his wife... This is my mobile... Can I take a message...? Very well... No, no it's no problem...

She resumes the dinner preparations, a little overexcited. Her mobile rings again.

Victoria (*even more annoyed*) – Hello...? *(Pleasant)* Oh hi John... No, no I'm fine… Did I tell you I quit smoking...? Well since this morning... No I'm not pregnant don't worry… But I had a two pack a day habit. Given the cost of cigarettes, in a year I'll have saved enough for a safari in Kenya. If I last just one week I can still get a bus pass. Just with the two packs I saved today I bought a large jar of Nutella… (*sighing*) I didn't think it would be so hard... What can I say... Even the cemetery is a no-smoking zone now… Dave is good. Until something better comes along… No I mean his job… Look, I have to go, my roast pork is drying in the oven. Speak to you soon? Ta ta…

Victoria hangs up, sniffs the air and turns towards the audience, worried.

Victoria – Can I smell gas…?

She runs to the kitchen to check on the roast pork. Dave, an educated middle-class man, comes in from the street whistling, wearing a raincoat and The Independent tucked under his arm. He removes his raincoat, sits on the sofa and thumbs through The Independent *whose first page reads: Mobile Phones Linked to Cancer? As Victoria comes out of the kitchen he quickly drops the paper on the table and makes a tragic face.*

Victoria (*happily*) – Hi!

Dave (*despondent*) – Hi...

Victoria (*noticing his face*) – Is something wrong?

Dave – I'm going to be laid off...

Victoria – Laid off! Why?

Dave – They're relocating...

Victoria – Oh no... I'm so sorry...

He collapses on the sofa.

Dave (*pathetic*) – You aren't going to leave me, are you?

Victoria comes to the sofa and takes him in her arms to comfort him.

Victoria – What are you talking about? I still have a job! Look, I even quit smoking. With the savings we'll make you'll be able to work part time – well almost. And if we have to tighten our belts, we'll tighten our belts. (*With a hand on her belly)* I'll quit Nutella.

Dave (*hamming it up)* – I don't want to be a burden… I'd rather end it all right now…

Victoria – What are you talking about…? We're married, Dave! For better or for worse! We'll just save the better for later... But it's crazy that they decide to relocate just like that without notice...

Dave – Nothing is safe from decentralisation.

Victoria – Yes but still... relocating the British Library... Where are they going to put it? It's rather a large building.

Dave – China... They're going to crate it all up and then rebuild it in a commercial zone outside Beijing. They have already started taking apart one of the reading rooms.

Victoria (*horrified*) – Really?

Dave – Yes...

Victoria – But what are the Chinese going to do with all those books? They can't read them! They won't even be able to alphabetise them...

Dave – They are going to use computer programmes to translate the entire English body of literature into Esperanto and then they'll digitise everything and store it in a huge central computer shaped like a pagoda. And of course, to access the data you'll need to pay a subscription, like Netflix.The paper will be recycled. At least it will save the last acres of eucalyptus forest left in China. (*Sighing*) If my sacrifice means a few pandas can be saved...

Victoria (*devastated*) – I can't believe it...

Dave tries to keep his composure a little longer, but breaks into laughter

Dave – I'm kidding! I'm kidding! Did you actually believe this nonsense?

Victoria, feeling both furious and relieved hits him with the sofa cushions.

Victoria – You shouldn't be joking about that...

Dave – You're right, it's not the right time to lose my job. It's rather well paid... and it gives me plenty of time to write... Speaking of which, I have good news to share. Strictly Confidential Publications have agreed to publish my play!

Victoria (*faking excitement)* – Strictly Confidential? Wow!

Dave – Yes... Well... At the author's expense... So I have to sell at least four thousand copies to recoup the publishing costs... Four thousand copies, that's doable, right?

Victoria – Sure, if you include your parents and mine... and if they take a thousand each!

Dave rubs his hands together with a satisfied smile.

Dave – Right, let's eat? It's Strip Poker tonight...

Victoria (*confused but possibly tempted*) – You want to play strip poker?

Dave – No, you know... Strip Poker, the reality show on TV!

Victoria – No...

Dave – They get couples together and every time one of them chooses to not answer the question asked by their spouse they take off a piece of clothing.

Victoria (*sighing*) – I don't understand how you can watch these stupid shows...

Dave – Oh, come on... it's the final tonight!

Victoria – Yes well final or not it's not going to happen...

Dave – The TV is broken?

Victoria – No… but you aren't going to be able to watch it…

Dave – You're revoking my television privileges…?

Dave notices the table, set for four.

Dave – Don't tell me you've invited your parents?

Victoria – The neighbours.

Dave – The neighbours? But they left a month ago...

Victoria – The new neighbours!

Dave – The new neighbours? But we don't even know them!

Victoria – Exactly. I bumped into the woman when I was taking down the rubbish... I thought it would be a good opportunity to meet them.

Dave – What for?

Victoria – Just to get to know them.

Dave – To get to know them for what?

Victoria – It's always a good idea to get to know your neighbours... You never know when you might need favours...

Dave – Favours...? What kind of favours?

Victoria – I don't know... Water the plants when we're not here...

Dave – Your cat ate the only plant I had in my office, last Sunday when we were having lunch with your parents.

Victoria – Well, there you go! If we had had someone to feed my cat, he wouldn't have eaten your plant. Speaking of which, I haven't seen the cat all day... strange...

Dave sighs.

Dave (*worried*) – They have children, don't they?

Victoria – Three, I think...

Dave – Don't tell me you invited them too?

Victoria – I'm sure they'd rather stay at home. (*Ironically*) They won't want to miss the Strip Poker final…

Dave – Rub it in, why don't you…?

Victoria – And they're just next door…

Dave – You weren't talking about the neighbours across the street?

Victoria – The neighbours across the street killed themselves six months ago! Remember all those fire engines, in the middle of the night? Flashing lights? Sirens?

Dave – No...

Victoria – It woke me up. I've had nightmares since... they turned on the gas... they almost blew up the whole block.

Dave – Some people are so selfish... Why did they kill themselves like that? Together?

Victoria – Go figure... Maybe there was nothing good on TV that evening... (*hinting*) Maybe if we had asked them over...

Dave (*can't believe her bad faith*) – Don't tell me you've invited the neighbours tonight so you don't feel guilty if they decide to kill themselves later?

She shrugs.

Victoria – Oh, by the way, I've been getting phone calls for you on my mobile all day.

Dave – Oh right, sorry, I don't know where I left mine… So I left your number on my answering machine at the office… In case a producer tries to reach me, for my play… It's best if they can reach me at all times… you understand...

Victoria (*astounded*) – My mobile number? Wouldn't it have been easier to just buy another phone?

Dave – Hmmm… At the end of the day you can live just fine without a mobile, don't you think?

Victoria – Sure… when you have a wife on receptionist duty.

Dave – Look, you decided to quit smoking, I decided to quit mobiles. Let's see who breaks first.

Victoria (*exasperated*) – But I don't ask you to smoke them for me!

Instead of replying, Dave goes back to reading The Independent. The audience can see the headline (Mobiles Linked to Cancer?) but Victoria can't. She looks at him, infuriated.

Victoria – Are you going to change before they get here?

Dave – Who?

Victoria – The neighbours!

Dave – Oh right, I forgot about that...

Dave, resigned, stands up to go change.

Victoria – I'm going to check in the kitchen in case the stove turned itself off. I think I can smell gas, can you?

Dave shrugs and leaves the room in the direction of the bedroom. Victoria also leaves but returns a few moments later with bottles and glasses to prepare drinks. Dave joins her shortly after in a very relaxed outfit.

Victoria (*not believing her eyes*) – You changed into your pyjamas?

Dave – They're not pyjamas! They're... jogging bottoms for staying in.

Victoria – And your grandpa slippers, they're not slippers either…?

Dave – Look, if the goal is to get up close and personal with the neighbours, we might as well hit the ground running.

Victoria – What if he's wearing a three piece suit and she's wearing a frock?!… I didn't tell them we were having a slumber party.

He sighs and leaves. She continues to prepare the room. He comes back in a more suitable outfit.

Dave (*narky*) – Is this OK?

Victoria (*not overly thrilled)* – It'll do...

Dave looks at the mail on the coffee table.

Dave – Dramatic Publishing, Samuel French, Applause…

She looks at him quizzically.

Dave – I'm kidding, unfortunately... (*thumbing through the three envelopes)* Phone, electricity, water bill. (*Sighing*) It's triple word count, today.

Victoria (*to lift his spirits*) – Royal Mail may be on strike again… when that happens they prioritise the bills.

Victoria's mobile rings and she picks up.

Victoria – Yes…? (*With faked politeness*) No this is the reception but please hold, I'll put you right through. (*She hands him her mobile, at her wits end*) Your friend, Patrick.

He takes the mobile as if nothing had happened.

Dave – Hi Patrick... How are you... Yes long time no see… Tuesday? Sure, why not... Hang on, I need to check with Victoria. She's busy right now. Can you call me back tomorrow? And um, if I'm not at home, try the mobile...

Exasperated look from Victoria.

Dave – Right, bye then...

He hangs up.

Dave – What a dick.

Victoria – What did he want?

Dave – We're invited for dinner Tuesday. It's his wife's birthday.

Victoria – I thought he was your best friend...?

Dave – Birthdays depress me... You don't see me inviting him to your birthdays, do you?

Victoria – You'd have to remember the date for that...

Dave – Really I would be much better off without a mobile. Right, what are they doing, these neighbours of ours... they can't say they were held up by traffic, they live across the street!

Victoria – Next door...

Dave – Even better, they don't even have to cross the road!

Victoria – It's not that bad, it's not that late...

Dave – Normally we'd have finished dinner by now. I'm getting really hungry... (*Surprised*) Especially since something smells so good. (*Curious*) What did you make?

Victoria (*proudly*) – Roast pork with prunes. I found the recipe in *Marie Claire*.

Dave – Hum... Are you sure this is the best time to try out new recipes?

He pauses.

Dave – I don't even know their names.

Victoria – She is Pam and he is James, I think.

Dave – Oh, I see you're already best mates... What's their last name?

Victoria (*thinking*) – I can't remember... it's like a brand of washing powder…

Dave – Daz?

Victoria shakes her head.

Dave – Persil?

Victoria shakes her head again.

Dave – Please tell me it's not Fairy.

Victoria (*finally remembering*) – Ariel! (*Not so sure anymore*) Or Mariel...

Dave – Wait, which is it Mariel or Ariel?

Victoria – I don't know. She said "Hello! My name is Pamariel"… we'll find out soon enough. Does it matter?

Dave – Well hello! If it's Ariel your roast pork isn't going to have much success… I guess they can still eat the prunes. One of their five a day.

Victoria (*horrified*) – I hadn't thought of that...

Dave – That's what happens when you invite people you don't know…

Victoria – How was I supposed to know? James and Pam that's not...

Dave – Not all Muslims aren't called Mohamed.

Victoria – You think they're Muslims?

Dave – Even if they were it wouldn't make any difference for the roast pork.

Victoria – Maybe they lapsed...

Dave – You should probably start defrosting a pizza... preferably a vegetarian one…

Victoria sighs. The doorbell rings. She freezes, panicked.

Victoria – What do we do?

Dave – I think you should open the door. That's usually what one does when one has invited guests and they are at the door... (*hopeful*) Or we turn off all the lights and we watch Strip Poker in the bathroom.

Victoria – I'll get it.

She disappears in the hallway to open the door and greet the neighbours.

Victoria (*off*) – Good evening... Come in... Welcome... (*taking what the neighbours are handing over*) Oh you shouldn't have, you really shouldn't have...

Dave (*aside, sighing*) – And the soap opera begins...

Victoria returns to the living room with a bunch of flowers, followed by the neighbours.

Dave (*mimicking Victoria's forced politeness*) – Hello, good evening... How do you do, how do you do…?

Victoria – What are they? Daisies? Look at those enormous petals!

Pam (*uncomfortable)* – They're tulips...

Victoria – Of course, they're beautiful!

Pam – I think they suffered a little heat stroke...

The flowers are indeed seriously flabby.

Victoria – I'll put them in water right away...

Dave – It might bring them back to life...

The neighbours step into the living room. Pam is a slim brunette, middle aged but still very attractive, dressed smartly but strictly with a suit and bun. James, chubby and heavy set, carries a bottle and wears a suit as flabby as the flowers. They are a conventional-looking couple and stand out next to the younger and more relaxed Dave and Victoria. Victoria makes the introductions.

Victoria (*to James*) – This is my husband (*stressing the surname*) Dave Gammon...

Both husbands shake hands.

Dave (*sinister*) – Happy to meet you...

Victoria (*to James*) – And you are…?

James (*smiling*) – James...

Victoria – Just James, very well...

James hands the bottle to Dave.

James – You should put it in the fridge...

Dave – Blue Nun Sparkling Wine…! Thank you so much James.

James – Served chilled they say it tastes just like Champagne.

Dave (*sarcastic*) – So why go for the real thing? I'll pop it in the freezer... that way it'll taste even better...

Dave takes the bottle to the kitchen.

Victoria (*embarrassed*) – Did you find it easy?

The look on the face of the neighbours who live next door.

Victoria (*back pedalling*) – No, I know you live next door... I mean, umm... Did you have trouble finding... (*ad-libbing*) a babysitter for your children?

Pam – Oh yes! The oldest watches the others... And if it's OK with you we might pop back later to check...

Dave returns.

Victoria – What are your children's names?

Pam – Sarah, Esther and the youngest is Benjamin.

Victoria visibly tries, and fails, to work out the neighbours' religious affiliations.

Victoria – Benjamin... of course... the youngest...

Pam – Am I right in thinking you don't have any children...?

Short, uneasy silence.

Victoria – Not yet... (*Diving in*) I'm sorry but your surname, is it Mariel like the first name or Ariel...?

Dave – Like the washing powder...

James – Mariel...

Victoria (*relieved*) – Whew! We were afraid you might be Jewish!

The guests are appalled. Victoria, horrified, corrects herself.

Victoria – I'm so sorry, it's just that I made roast pork... but we'll find something. I'm sure I have a pizza in the bottom of the freezer... it won't be anything fancy...

Dave – Or we can take a rain check...

Victoria glares at him.

Pam (*relaxing a little*) – Oh, don't change anything for our benefit. Roast pork will be just fine...

James (*deadpan*) – However, the prunes... are they kosher? (*satisfied with Victoria's embarrassed look*) I'm kidding... as long as they're stoned! Like I always say, it's better for your teeth... What's your surname again? Bacon?

Victoria – Gammon...

James – Oh, shame.

Neither Dave nor Victoria get it.

James (*pleased with himself*) – Because, you know... David and Victoria Bacon... (*the others still don't get it*) David and Victoria Beckham!

Pam doesn't find the joke funny either.

Victoria (*forcing a smile*) – I am happy to see you have a good sense of humour... and after all, Jewish or Muslim what's the difference?

Dave – Exactly, it could have been worse! You could have been a dentist or in IT...

Another uncomfortable silence...

Victoria (*to break the awkwardness*) – Drinks anyone?

Blackout.

ACT TWO

Both couples are nursing drinks. Dave and Victoria are already bored shitless but are actively listening to James' dull stories.

James – The problem is that dentists today spend more and more time filling in paperwork than filling teeth. And since everything is done on computers nowadays... Like I always say, they taught me to use a drill, not a mouse. I'm lucky that my wife can help me. IT is her job, but for me…

Dave and Victoria nod politely.

James – I mean really, today private medical professionals are crushed by corporate taxes… Speaking of which, stop me if you've heard this one.

Dave and Victoria take on a politely interested look.

James – A dentist is on a cruise in the Pacific Ocean with his wife. They get shipwrecked. The ship sinks…

Victoria burst out laughing. The other three are confused.

James – I'm not done...

Victoria composes herself.

James – They drift for a week before washing up ashore a deserted island. Naturally, the wife is very worried. She says to her husband: they'll never find us!

Victoria bursts out laughing again.

James – I'm still not done...

Victoria composes herself once more.

James – The husband asks: did you pay HMRC before we left? His wife: no! Her husband says: then don't worry, they'll find us!

James guffaws loudly at his own joke. Victoria, burned, doesn't laugh.

James – Now I'm done...

Victoria forces a stupid smile. James pulls out a pack of cigarettes and offers it to Dave.

James – Cigarette?

Dave – I don't smoke, thanks...

James turns the pack towards Victoria.

Victoria – I quit this morning…

Pam glares at James who puts the pack away.

James – OK, I won't subject you to passive smoking then... You know, they say about how bad cigarettes are but mobiles aren't much better for your health, are they? I read an article in The Independent this morning. Apparently after 15 minutes a day you're pretty much guaranteed a brain tumour.

Victoria, intrigued, takes The Independent that Dave brought from the coffee table and reads the headline: Mobiles Linked to Cancer?

James – You better not use all your minutes!

Victoria glares at Dave who looks innocent.

James – I smoke but I don't have a mobile!

Victoria (*sarcastic*) – My husband either. He'd rather I get the tumour for him...

James – Do you know the most annoying part of my job?

Dave and Victoria pretend to think about it.

James – Washing your hands all the time, in between patients. Look at my hands. They're desiccated! I could wear gloves, but... can you imagine... it's very fine work, dentistry. Have you ever tried to thread a needle with boxing gloves?

Dave – Never... Actually I sew very little... I prefer knitting myself…

James – It's like I always say, us dentists we have it better than shrinks: my patients also lie down and open their mouth... but they have to listen to me!

Pam – You're boring everyone with your stories…

Victoria – Not at all…!

Pam – Why don't you tell us a little about you... (*to Victoria*) You're a teacher, is that right?

Victoria – I teach music theory… but I'm not sure it's more interesting…

Dave makes a face that she has put her foot in her mouth again.

Pam – Ah, music theory… I did that for more than 10 years when I was young…

Victoria (*trying to look interested*) – You played an instrument?

Pam – I wish… My parents must have thought that music theory was to be learned like classical languages. Like Latin or Greek. So when I turned 18 I out my food down and said enough.

Dave (*feigning to be impressed*) – Wow, you sure were a rebellions teen…

Pam – Then I signed up for ballroom dancing classes.

Victoria – That's quite a change…

James (*tenderly*) – That's where we met.

Victoria (*feigning interest*) – Really?

James – Believe it or not I used to be a very good dancer… Still not too shabby now if I say so myself… Apparently 40% of men meet their future spouse by asking them to dance… (*to Dave*) Is that how you met your beautiful wife?

Dave – Not at all… I ravished her savagely in a back alley on a stormy day after offering my umbrella… Apparently it's quite an unusual way to meet one's future spouse...

Embarrassed silence.

Victoria – My husband is joking of course…

Dave – She hates it when I tell that story…

Victoria – Would you like another drink?

Pam – Well… maybe a finger…

Dave – Before or after the drink?

Victoria throws daggers at Dave and refills her guests' glasses.

Pam – We enrolled Benjamin, our youngest, in the infant school next door… Do you know whether it has good reputation?

Victoria – I don't know, I don't have children.

Pam – Oh that's right. I'm sorry…

Dave – Well, it's not really your fault, is it?

Silence.

Pam – How about you Dave? What do you do for a living…

Dave – Me? Nothing...

The neighbours make an appropriate face.

Pam (*sympathetic*) – On the dole…?

Dave – Oh no, I don't scrounge… I'm more of an… inactive employee. It's very difficult to get to the point where you look like you're working when you don't have anything to do. You have to be a very good actor.

Pam (*awkward*) – Well… what do you do when you're not working…? I mean, when you are not in the office?

Dave – Actually, I am an actor! Well, part time anyway…

Pam (*intrigued*) – An actor? I knew you looked familiar… Have I seen you in anything?

Dave – Do you watch Loose Women?

James (*impressed*) – Sure, sometimes! It's on when I take my nap...

Dave – Have you seen the ad for funeral protection plans that comes on just before?

James doesn't look like he has.

Dave – You know the one… it comes on after the advert for hearing aids and before the one for stair lifts.

James – Um... maybe...

Dave – I'm the man in the casket.

James (*disconcerted*) – Really…?

Dave – Not so much a bit part as a body part...

Victoria glares at Dave, who is very proud of himself.

Pam (*embarrassed*) – And aside from that, are you working on anything else…?

The doorbell rings.

James – Are you waiting for more guests?

Victoria – No, no... We're not expecting anyone else...

Dave goes to open the door.

Dave (*off*) – Already?... Excuse me, I'll be right back…

Dave comes back with a box full of poppies.

Dave (*awkward*) – It's the Scouts, selling poppies for Remembrance Day...

Dave – Wow, they're really early this year… are you sure it's a real Scout?

Dave – Well, he's wearing a Scout uniform and looks a lot like the boy who sells us poppies every year.

James – Oh...

Dave – You wouldn't happen to have a tenner would you? I don't have any change. I'll pay you back after he leaves.

James, reluctantly searches his pockets.

James – You know what... I used my last fiver to buy the wine. I have a quid or two if you want...

Dave – Right... I'm going to give him the bottle then... You don't mind, do you?

James – Not at all... Go ahead...

Dave hands James the box of poppies.

Dave – You get to pick one then...

While Dave goes to find the bottle of wine in the kitchen, James pulls out his reading glasses and looks at the poppies with affected seriousness.

James – I think I like this one with the felt petals... it's nice... what do you think, Pam?

Pam doesn't reply. Dave returns with the bottle of sparkling wine.

Dave – You can keep the poppy of course… since the Scout is taking your bottle.

James – Thank you...

Dave leaves with the box of poppies and the bottle of sparkling wine.

Dave (*off*) – Here you go... it's nice and cold... Lest we forget...

Dave returns.

Pam – Poppies... in September... the cheek...

Dave – Must be global warming... all the seasons feel the same... even the Scouts can't tell.

Victoria – I'm going to check on my roast pork. I think I can smell gas...

James (*standing*) – I'm going to pop back home to check on the kids. Before we sit down for dinner...

Victoria – Of course...

James – Please don't get up, I know the way.

Pam (*standing as well*) – Could you show me where to wash my hands... It's the nuts... It's always a little greasy...

Victoria – Sure, straight down the hall...

James and Pam leave the room.

Victoria – Why on Earth did you tell them you played a corpse in a funeral plan advert? (*Mocking Dave*) Not so much a bit part as a body part...

Dave – Look, I was trying to set the mood because this party isn't exactly getting started, is it? And we haven't even started the meal yet... I won't last until dessert, I'm warning you... We have to come up with something to make them leave...

Victoria – I know, they're not very interesting... But it's too late to cancel. We won't invite them again, that's all.

Dave – But don't you realise they're going to want to return the invitation…? It won't be that easy to end this relationship. You've started a chain of events, can't you see?

Victoria understands, but tries to minimise the problem.

Victoria – Oh come on... In any case, let's get this dinner going... Can you open the wine...?

Dave – At least I managed to get rid of his sparkling wine. It gives me gas…

Victoria leaves towards the kitchen. Dave grabs the bottle of wine. Pam comes back.

Pam – It's really nice to make the effort to meet us... I used to live in the area, a long time ago, when I was in high school, but I don't know anyone any more... Also, you never know when you might need a helping hand from your neighbours.

Dave – That's what my wife says... (*He gets an idea*) Speaking of which, I'm glad you said that... Because I have something I wanted to ask you.

Dave hands over the bottle.

Dave – Do you mind opening it? I don't think I have the strength...

Pam, intrigued, tries to open the bottle clumsily. She deploys super human efforts to pull out the cork.

Dave – I didn't want to dampen the evening, but... I have cancer...

Pam pulls out the cork violently. Dave catches the bottle and starts pouring while he shares more information.

Dave – I just found out I had a tumour… I must have used all my minutes and then some…

Pam – Your minutes…?

Dave – My mobile phone minutes… the… um… radiations. It must have been an old model…

Pam (*compassionate*) – Your brain…

Dave – Worse…

Pam stares, wondering what could be worse.

Dave – The testicles…

Pam (*horrified*) – No…!

Dave – Hands free kits, they keep radiation away from your head, but they just move the problem elsewhere…

Pam – I am so very sorry…

Dave (*raising his glass for a toast)* – Anyway, cheers… We shouldn't let this wine spoil…

They toast grimly.

Pam – But... Aren't there treatments nowadays…

Dave – Yes there are… actually my surgeon is considering a graft… (*Pregnant pause*) And that's the reason I wanted my wife to invite you over… You and your husband…

Pam is confused.

Dave – Another one?

Pam, in great need of an alcoholic pick-me-up agrees. He pours her a large glass that she drinks in one go.

Pam – Ah, that's the good stuff, isn't it?

Dave – Have some peanuts…

Pam helps herself.

Dave – So the thing is… I need a donor…

Pam – A donor…?

Dave comes close to her and puts his hand on her shoulders.

Dave – You can live perfectly well with a single testicle you know… The operation is quite safe and a week later you don't even think about it anymore. You can't even see the scar…

Pam (*puzzled*) – I mean… I'll have to talk to my husband… I don't know if…

Victoria returns and sees them in this awkward position.

Pam (*embarrassed*) – I'll go and check how James is doing with the children… You know men…

She leaves quickly.

Victoria – Well, it looks like you're getting friendly after all…

Dave – Oh please, it's a nightmare, we've got to find a way to get rid of them…

Victoria – What do you want to do? We can't throw them out, we invited them!

Dave – When you say "we"…

Victoria – OK, I made a mistake but now they're here… we have to see this through… Rats, I left the bread in the kitchen.

Before leaving for the kitchen, Victoria glances at a copy of Marie-Claire that is lying on a chair.

Victoria *(disappointed)* – It doesn't look as nice as it did in *Marie Claire...*

Dave – What doesn't?

Victoria – My roast pork!

Dave – Women in the street also don't look like *Marie Claire* models… I don't see why it should be any different for your roast pork.

Victoria shrugs and leaves, upset, but turns towards Dave before entering the kitchen.

Victoria – Please try and be nice…

Dave – So they feel welcome and stay even longer?

Victoria – They could be our neighbours for the next twenty years. We don't want to argue with them so soon after their arrival...

Dave (*despairing*) – But the best way to avoid arguing with the neighbours is to never speak to them…

Victoria is about to return to the kitchen but turns back for one last question.

Victoria – By the way, have you seen the cat?

Dave (*a little uncomfortable)* – Not since this morning…

Victoria – I hope your potted plant wasn't toxic.

Victoria leaves. James returns.

James – Pam is putting the youngest to bed. The other two are watching telly…

Dave – Strip Poker...?

James – Sophie's Choice... My favourite film... Yum... Something smells really good!

James puts both hands on Dave's shoulders.

James – I am sure we'll get along splendidly… And the good thing about dining next door is that you don't have to drive home... We can stay late... and not worry about alcohol tests!

Dave (*suddenly inspired*) – Tell me James... Can I call you James?

James – Of course, Dave. We're neighbours after all...

Dave – I feel we're getting along so well. I have a proposition for you. I should say we have a proposition, my wife and I.

James (*intrigued*) – Yes?

Dave – Have you heard of... swinging?

James (*dumbfounded*) – A little...

Dave – See, my wife and I… I mean, if you wanted… Don't feel like you have to. Usually it happens after the meal, before dessert… So if you aren't interested… Just make your excuses before we serve dessert. My wife and I will understand.

James, taken aback, doesn't have time to reply. Pam returns.

Pam – Well, that's done! Now nothing will interrupt our evening, just the four of us…

Pam notices the face James is making.

Pam – Is something wrong?

James (*embarrassed*) – No, no… We were talking… about open markets. Globalisation, decentralisation, all that stuff… Did you know that my wife is an ardent defender of open marriages…?

Pam (*correcting him, uncomfortable)* – Open markets...

Embarrassed silence. Victoria returns from the kitchen with the roast pork.

Victoria – Well, if you don't have any objection to eating pork, dinner is served...

They gather around the table, in an awkward silence.

Victoria – Pam, will you sit next to my husband…?

Pam does so while James looks on, worried. Victoria serves her guests.

Pam – This looks delicious…

Victoria is about to fill Dave's plate.

Dave – No thank you…

Victoria – You're not hungry?

Dave – Not really... and meat has always made me feel a little sick. Not you…?

James and Pam look at him, stunned.

Dave – Did you know that the pig is the animal that is genetically closest to Man? Only a handful of chromosomes separate us from pigs. (*Looking towards James*) Some of us even less so...

The guests, taken aback by the conversation, pick at their food with little appetite. Victoria tries to change the subject.

Victoria – What about you, Pam? You haven't told us what you did…

Pam – It's always delicate to say… It's not very popular these days…

Dave – Are you a stripper… or a car mechanic?

Pam – Worse… I am a… (*pompously*) Cost Killer.

Dave and Victoria do not understand.

James – Like a Head Hunter… but literally: she actually hunts the heads to cut them off.

Victoria – What do you do, exactly?

Pam – Well… Struggling companies ask me to consult with them to identify the dead wood that should be cut, so that the young, healthy branches can flourish…

James – It's like I always say, head hunting is actually the opposite of recruiting… My wife makes heads roll by cutting costs!

Victoria (*hand on her throat, impressed*) – It sounds very interesting…

James – My wife is the Che Guevara of the Liberal Revolution… an ardent defender of open marriages…

Pam (*correcting him*) – Open markets…

James – Um... yes, that's what I meant…

Victoria – And whose branches are you thinking of pruning with your chainsaw?

Pam – In the past I worked mostly with private companies. But recently I have been called upon to work with the public sector. In fact, I have just been given a new project...

Victoria (*trying to joke, a little worried*) – Don't tell me you're going to work for the Board of Education… Because I imagine that music theory teachers will be the first to get the chop...

Pam – You're joking but it's probably going to happen eventually. Right now it's another dinosaur that I have been asked to tear apart.

Victoria – Not the Labour Party?

Pam (*looking pleased with herself*) – The British Library…

Dave chokes.

Dave – The British Library…!

Pam – Obviously, this is strictly between us… I start tomorrow morning and no one knows about this yet. I will identify which employees are the most productive… The rest will be replaced with computers…

James – My wife is a killer. In the trade they call her Osama. When she's done with the British Library they won't need the reading room any longer.

Victoria is speechless and Dave is about to pass out. Their guests don't notice anything.

Pam – I am boring you with my stories… The roast pork is truly delicious. Will you give me the recipe?

James stands up.

James – Excuse me… I need to use the bathroom before the next course… Must be the prunes…

Pam – Good idea… I'll go check on the children, make sure they haven't found a way to watch dirty movies on cable, even though we don't get cable.

While James and Pam are away.

Dave (*crestfallen*) – That's it. I am sure to get the chop. I'll be in the first batch…

Victoria – Why did you have to brag about not doing anything…? (*Mocking him*) You need to be a very good actor…

Dave (*outraged*) – Hang on! How was I supposed to know she was a Cost Killer? She looked tame enough… And you invited her! If you had told me that we were having Mrs Pol Pot for dinner I would have been more circumspect…

Victoria – I don't know how to make things up…

Dave – Especially since I just suggested a foursome after dinner…

Victoria – Excuse me?

Dave – It was meant to make them leave early…

Victoria (*hurt*) – Gee, thanks… So not only is she going to think you are a parasite but also a pervert… And what if they had agreed?

Dave – I only spoke to her husband… Actually he didn't say no… And since now we have to do everything we can to make them stay and fix this…

Victoria, about to have a nervous breakdown, lights a cigarette.

Victoria – This wasn't the day to quit.

Victoria inhales deeply.

Victoria (*sensual*) – Ah, this feels good...

Dave looks at her, unsettled, then regains control.

Dave – Right, listen, at this point there's only one thing we can do...

Victoria – Turn on the gas, like the neighbours across the street?

Dave – She doesn't know I work for the British Library yet... We have to use the rest of the evening to find something we can hold against her.

Victoria – And how are you going to do that? You're not thinking of asking me to go along with the pervy proposition you made to her husband just so you can blackmail them and keep your job?

Dave – Hopefully not if we can avoid it... For starters maybe we can make her drink… She's got to have something to hide, little miss goody two shoes.

Victoria – Get her drunk…? You really think that's all it will take to get her to jump on the table and make a public confession Cultural Revolution-style…? No, to make her confess… Apart from sticking her head in the oven, I can't see how… (*Day dreaming*) I could lure her in the kitchen while you stall her husband...

Dave isn't listening and continues his train of thought...

Dave – A public confession... I have an idea...

Victoria – Yes…?

Dave – Strip Poker!

Victoria – What now? You want to play strip poker with them?

Dave – Strip Poker, the TV show! When she's nice and drunk we suggest to play the same game.

Victoria (*worried*) – What same game?

Dave – The player who forfeits has to answer an embarrassing question. Like truth or dare! She's a player. With a few drinks down her I'm sure she'll be up for it.

Victoria (*worried*) – But I don't know how to play poker…

Dave (*surprised*) – Do you have anything to hide?

Victoria – Not really, but...

Dave – Well there you go! Nothing to worry about.

James and Pam come back.

James – Ah, I feel better!

Victoria – So, who's ready for dessert…?

James is visibly embarrassed.

James – It's getting late, isn't it? We don't want to impose...

Pam (*surprised*) – Come on James, we can't leave like that...

Dave, desperate to get them to stay to fix things, changes behaviour entirely.

Dave (*friendly*) – But you aren't imposing at all! After dessert we can play a party game together… Do you like games?

Pam – Oh my, you've found my weak spot! I love playing games... don't I, James?

Blackout.

ACT THREE

The scene is like a smoky bar. All four are sitting around a poker table, smoking and bedraggled. The table is lit with a lamp like in films. As James and Pam look on, impressed, Victoria shuffles the deck with the ease of a casino croupier.

Dave – So, is everything clear for everyone? At the end of each game, the player with the most buttons can ask a question to the player with the least buttons…

The others nod their head yes.

James (*trying to joke*) – As long as it's not the buttons holding my trousers. Apart from what they're covering I don't have anything to hide…

Dave (*threatening*) – We all have something to hide… if you look hard enough… You just need to ask the right questions…

The atmosphere is heavier. The game starts. The four players bet. James cuts the deck. Victoria deals the cards (five each) and Dave pushes a bottle towards Pam.

Dave – Another night cap…?

Pam (*already tipsy*) – Go on then, if you can't overdo it once in a while…

James – Are you sure this is reasonable? (*Trying to joke*) Did you know that you are now legally responsible if you let your guests leave drunk…

Dave – But you said so yourself: you don't have to drive anywhere. You live across the street…

James – Next door…

Dave – See, you won't even risk getting run over crossing the road… (*Hinting at James*) But if you'd rather stay the night with us…

James looks embarrassed.

Pam (*finishing her drink bottoms up*) – Ah… You can really taste the pear…!

James' smile freezes. Victoria finished dealing the cards. They all look at their cards, and at each other.

Dave – Two…

Victoria deals his cards.

Pam – Three…

James – One…

Victoria – Served…

They look at their new hand. They look at each other surreptitiously. And they take turn speaking.

Dave – I fold…

James – Me too…

Pam – I'll raise you two.

Victoria – To see.

Pam shows her cards with childish excitement.

Pam – Four aces! Anyone got better?

Victoria (*grim*) – Three jacks...

Pam takes the pot. Everyone looks at the buttons in front of them.

Pam – I get to ask a question...

The others count their buttons, uneasy. Victoria's face falls when she realises she has the least.

Pam – To Victoria!

Dave and James are visibly relieved.

Pam – You have to tell the truth…

Victoria (*worried*) – Go ahead…

Pam – Have you ever shoplifted, in a store?

Victoria is almost relieved.

Victoria – Yes… Once… A tent…

James – You attempted to steal something?

Victoria – No! A tent, as in 'camp'!

Pam – A camp man?

Victoria – A tent to go camping!

James – Oh... I wouldn't have thought you could steal something like that! It's rather bulky, isn't it, a tent?

Pam – A tent…? Was it... out of necessity? Did you need somewhere to sleep...

Victoria – It was to go camping! I was in a shopping centre… I went to the till to pay. They told me to go to another till and I realised I had walked right out of the store, straight through the security barriers, without noticing. Since I was already outside…

Dave – Technically that's not stealing… Since you didn't have the intention to steal this tent...

Victoria – I didn't go back to pay for it... I was actually afraid that I'd trigger the security barriers walking back in. It would have been really stupid to get caught while trying to sneak the tent I had stolen by accident back in the store to pay for it... Can you imagine trying to explain this to the security guards? They don't look like they have that kind of imagination...

Faces of the others picturing the situation.

Pam – Was that the only time?

Victoria – Yes...

Pam – You're quite an honest woman then...

Victoria – You know, most people are honest because they don't have the courage to be dishonest... For me the risk always appeared greater than the benefits...

James (*loosened up by alcohol*) – Like cheating on your husband…?

Victoria – I think that counts as a second question...

James – You're right…

A new game starts. Same thing. They bet. Dave deals the cards.

Pam – One…

James – Nothing…

Victoria – Nothing…

Dave – Two please…

They bet again.

Pam – Call…

James – I'll raise you one…

Victoria – I fold…

Dave – I'll see you…

They show their cards.

Dave (*triumphantly*) – Full house!

James – Flush!

Dave's smile freezes. Victoria looks at him ironically.

Victoria – Well… that's a good start…

James takes all the buttons in the pot.

James – My turn to ask a question…

The others are on the defensive, counting their buttons.

James – To Dave… *(Dave looks defeated)* Have you ever had the desire to kill someone?

Dave – Before tonight you mean?

James – And actually started to execute the plan, of course… Or it doesn't count… If we locked up all the husbands who wanted to kill their wives more than once a week… the prisons are already overpopulated.

Pam throws daggers at him. Dave tries to remember.

Dave – No, I don't think so… Actually… well it wasn't premeditated but… In high school… there was this fat chick with glasses we would pick on. One day at the pool we threw her glasses in the deep end. She couldn't swim. But in her panic she forgot. She jumped in to get her glasses back. We were laughing like hyenas. Of course, after several minutes, when we didn't see her come back up, we called the life guard… It was hilarious… I can't remember this poor girl's name…

Pam – Pam Robert...

Dave (*stunned*) – Yes, actually...

Pam – The fat chick with glasses. That was me…

Dave – Really…?!

Pam – I was sure I knew you from somewhere…

James steps in to lighten the atmosphere.

James – Right, let's play another round.

Another round is started. Without enthusiasm. And in a heavy silence. Pam deals.

James – Fold.

Victoria – Served...

Dave – I fold too.

Pam – Raising you ten…

Victoria – I'll see your ten and raise twenty…

Pam (*betting*) – Call.

Pam and Victoria show their hand. Victoria's satisfied smile. Pam's decomposed face.

Victoria – Ha, this time it's my turn to ask a question… to Pam…

Pam is worried.

Victoria – Have you ever committed a grave professional mistake, one that you've never told anyone about?

Pam is deeply unsettled. She walks to the front of the stage as if for a confession. But instead of talking, she removes her top.

Blackout.

The lights come back and Pam is still in the hot seat, at the front of the stage. She has lost another game.

Victoria – Same question as before… Have you ever committed a grave professional mistake…?

Pam is about to remove her skirt... but she changes her mind and speaks in a voice barely audible.

Pam (*very quietly*) – Yes…

Victoria – I'm sorry?

Pam – Yes!

Victoria – Tell us more.

Pam – Well... It won't leave this room...? Promise…?

Dave and Victoria nod hypocritically.

Dave – We might as well be in church taking your confession…

The smoky dive atmosphere is far from that image.

James (*bemused*) – A church…?

Victoria – Or a synagogue if you prefer.

Pam – They have confessions in synagogues?

Dave (*impatiently*) – I don't know... Pretend you're on Jeremy Kyle...

Pam – OK then... It was six months ago, give or take... During one of my interventions I had a manager and his partner fired. They both worked in the company I was auditing… I was sure they were stealing from the company… He couldn't take it. He had been working in that company for twenty years. He killed himself… and his wife…

Dave and Victoria exchange a satisfied look. They now have enough to compromise Pam.

Pam – He gassed them both…

Dave (*aghast*) – The neighbours from across the street…!

Pam – I'm sorry?

Dave – Never mind...

Pam – I realised they were innocent right after the funeral… I had made a mistake adding up the numbers… I didn't tell anyone… I didn't do anything to restore their good name... I am so ashamed... (*in tears*) I never make mistakes adding up numbers...

James is comforting her.

James (*to Dave and Victoria*) – She always gets upset when we talk about this… (*Trying to console his wife*) Do you want to go home, honey…?

Dave and Victoria share a look showing they agree with that decision, since they now have what they need.

Victoria – Yes, maybe we've had enough…

Pam (*chin up*) – No, no, I don't want to ruin the evening… I'll be fine… (*Hoping for her revenge*) Besides, you don't quit a poker game just like that… (*With a worrying look*) Some of us have yet to answer questions…

Pam finishes her drink in one go to drown her remorse.

Dave – Let's go…

James deals the cards... They start playing in silence. The atmosphere is heavier by the minute.

Victoria – One…

Dave – Served…

Pam – Raise…

James – To see…

They reveal their cards on the table.

Pam – Two Jacks…

James – Three tens…

Victoria – Four sixes…

Dave (*triumphantly*) – Four kings!

The others are uneasy.

Dave – James…

James keeps his poker face.

Dave – Do you know what happened to the cat I saw near the bins this morning…

Victoria is dumbfounded. James and Pam are uncomfortable.

Dave – You have to tell the truth…

James moves to the front of the stage as if to start a confession. Instead of speaking he takes off his trousers revealing boxer shorts.

Blackout.

The lights come back on and James is still being questioned at the front of the stage. We understand that he lost a second time.

Dave – So, about the cat?

James is about to remove his boxer shorts but Pam answers for him.

Pam – He had already eaten three of the potted plants on the balcony... so I watered the fourth one with arsenic.

Victoria bursts into tears.

Dave – Oh my god! These words are razors to my wounded heart...

General unease.

James (*to break up the tension*) – One last game? Give me a chance to win it back…

Pam – Sure, but then we'll all go to bed.

The look on the faces of the others who aren't sure what to make of her last comment.

A new game. The players bet. Victoria deals the cards again. The players bet more. Everyone's face shows even more tension than before.

Dave – One.

Pam – One.

James – Served.

Victoria – One.

James bets all his buttons.

James – All in!

Victoria – Fold...

Dave – Fold...

Pam – Me too...

James collects the pot. His face lights up. Victoria realises with horror that she has the least buttons.

James – My turn to ask a question...

Victoria (*panicked*) – But you didn't show us your hand…!

James – I don't have to! You all folded!

He looks at the other three in turn to keep up the suspense.

James – Victoria has the fewest buttons… So here goes…

Victoria is very uncomfortable.

James (*without pity*) – Have you ever cheated on your husband?

Victoria is speechless. Dave looks at her, worried.

Pam – Come on, we all had to answer. You have to tell the truth...

Victoria walks to the front of the stage. She removes her top.

Blackout.

Light.

James (*without pity*) – Have you ever cheated on your husband?

Victoria, increasingly uncomfortable, removes her skirt and is now wearing a slip.

Blackout.

Light.

James (*without pity*) – Have you ever cheated on your husband?

Victoria goes to remove her slip but chooses to answer instead.

Victoria – Once... Just once... It was... a mistake.

Dave is aghast.

Pam (*cruelly*) – A mistake? Like the tent?

Victoria – In a way...

James (*hammering it in*) – No really... You don't end up with the wrong partner like you dial a wrong number.

Pam – And even if you do dial a wrong number you can always hang up without starting a conversation...

Victoria – Let's say that hanging up didn't come to mind... I am very talkative on the phone...

Pam – Had you told your husband, before tonight?

Victoria – No...

Pam – Why not?

Victoria – I managed to walk out without triggering the security gates... and I didn't have the courage to go back and pay what I owed...

Unease. Dave and Victoria avoid looking at each other.

James – OK, well... Let's call it a night...

Dave (*to James*) – You were bluffing?

James, feeling very proud of himself, reveals his hand.

James – I only have a small pair...

Another silence. Pam and James leave the table and get ready to leave.

James (*to Dave)* – I have a last question to ask you...

Dave – The game is over.

James – But I showed you my pair...

Dave – Ask away...

James – Are you really an actor?

Dave – No, but I am a playwright. During my work hours… (*Looking at Pam*) at the British Library…

Pam – I see… Can I count on your discretion…?

Dave (*innocently*) – About the neighbours across the street...? If your report mentions that I am the most productive employee in the organisation, and that a computer couldn't possibly begin to fill my role…

Pam takes the blow.

Pam – Do you mind if I go get a glass of water from the kitchen? I don't feel so good…

Victoria – Please do…

Pam leaves for the kitchen.

James – Next time we'll have you over… We can play Scrabble, for a change…

Pam is back.

James – See you soon?

Dave (*to Pam*) – Maybe even tomorrow…?

They leave. Dave and Victoria are alone. They avoid looking at each other. They look around at the messy apartment.

Victoria's mobile phone starts ringing.

Dave – Aren't you going to answer?

Victoria – I don't even know if it's for me or for you. You gave my mobile number to all your friends…

Dave – Because I trust you…

Victoria is embarrassed.

Dave (*more seriously*) – Who was it… your wrong number?

Victoria (*cringing*) – John

Dave – Oh, wow… I wouldn't have thought he was a risk…

Victoria hugs Dave to ask for forgiveness.

Victoria – So, how about this strip poker now?

Dave – All in!

Moody music. She starts to strip. He is looking at her, turned on. He sits to watch her performance and pulls out a large cigar which he is about to light with a match he takes from a matchbox.

For a second the audience can glimpse Pam's face spying on them... she is wearing a gas mask from World War II over her face. Then she disappears.

Victoria stops abruptly, along with the music.

Victoria (*worried*) – Can you smell gas?

He waves off her concern and strikes the match for his cigar. Blackout followed by a bright flash and the sound of an explosion.

End.

November 2017

Made in the USA
Las Vegas, NV
01 May 2025